CHARTS AND GRAPHS

Karen Bryant-Mole
Illustrated by Graham Round

Edited by Kathy Gemmell
Series editor: Jenny Tyler

What are charts and graphs?

Charts and graphs are ways of showing information without writing it all out in words. Often this means drawing a picture of some sort to make the information easier to understand.

In this book you will meet a family called the Ogs. The Ogs live in Reptile Road, in Ogtown. They will help you find out about charts and graphs and what they can be used for.

Making a weather chart

Grandpa Og wants to know more about Ogtown's weather. He reads today's weather report and decides that it would be clearer to show the weather in pictures. He has used the information written in the report to draw the chart below.

Here is the forecast for the next day. See if you can help Grandpa Og fill in the blank chart, using the same symbols as he used in his first chart.

Today's weather report for Ogtown

Today it will be sunny in the east of the area.

The north and south will have a mixture of sunshine and showers.

It will rain in the west.

The wind is coming from the west so this means that the rain will spread toward the east as the day progresses.

Tomorrow's weather report

The day will begin with rain in the north and east.

It will be sunny in the south.

There will be a mixture of sunshine and showers in the west.

The wind will be coming from the south.

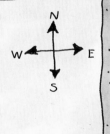

Tally sheets

Before you can make a chart or graph, you need to collect information.

Many of the charts and graphs in this book involve numbers. The information that is needed often answers the question, "How many?"

One of the best ways to record information like this is to use a type of chart called a tally sheet. You can see one below.

Zog and Mog's traffic tally sheet

cars	~~IIII~~ ~~IIII~~ ~~IIII~~ III
buses	IIII
bikes	~~IIII~~ IIII
trucks	~~IIII~~ ~~IIII~~ III

Zog and Mog Og wanted to find out more about the amount of traffic on Reptile Road. They decided to count all the traffic that passed.

Information is sometimes called **data**.

I wonder how many beetle juices are sold?

How many people can swim?

I'd like to know how many people like rockburgers.

Tally sheets are a quick way of collecting information and they are easy to understand.

As each vehicle passed by, Zog and Mog made a tally mark (which is just a small, straight line) in the correct row.

The tally marks are grouped in fives. The first four are drawn next to each other and the fifth crosses the first four.

18 cars and 4 buses went by. Can you see how many bikes and trucks went by and write the numbers in the boxes below?

Meet the Og family

Grandma Og

Grandma Og loves spiders. She can spot eighteen different types.

Grandpa Og

Grandpa Og enjoys butterfly watching. He particularly likes the Blobble butterfly.

Mrs. Og

Mrs. Og likes flower arranging. She thinks that yellow flowers make the best displays.

Mr. Og

Mr. Og is a dragonfly spotter. He likes the way the sun shines through their wings.

Mog Og

Mog has a pet lizard at home. She likes looking for wild lizards in the forest.

Zog Og

Zog likes anything that is red. He enjoys trying to find red flowers.

The Ogs are on a nature watch in Fern Forest. Zog suggests they all make tally sheets for the plants or animals they like best. As soon as they spot one of the things they like, they make a tally mark on their sheets.

Can you help the Ogs fill in their tally sheets?

In the café

Mog and Zog often go to the Tyrannosaurus Rex Café in Ogtown. It is owned by their friend, Mr. Trog.

There are only four things on the food menu and four things on the drinks menu in the T-Rex Café.

Mr. Trog likes to keep a count of all the items he sells. He thinks that he is a very good artist. Instead of making a tally sheet, he prefers to draw a picture of everything that he sells.

This is what Mr. Trog sold yesterday.

This sort of chart is called a **pictograph**.

Swamp-burger	
Bronto-burger	
T-Rex Steak	
Pterodactyl Pie	

What was the most popular meal?

How many swampburgers were sold?

If Mr. Trog wanted to change one of the meals on the menu, which do you think he should choose?

Food
Swampburger 17 pebbles
Brontoburger 19 pebbles
T-Rex Steak 25 pebbles
Pterodactyl Pie 16 pebbles

Drinks
Beetle juice 10 pebbles
Slug juice 9 pebbles
Glug juice 12 pebbles
Bug juice 11 pebbles

Mog and Zog decide to order a glass of juice. Mog has slug juice and Zog has glug juice.

So far today, including these drinks, Mr. Trog has sold 8 rock mugs of beetle juice, 4 rock mugs of slug juice, 7 rock mugs of glug juice and 10 rock mugs of bug juice.

Find some crayons and complete this pictograph by filling in the correct number of rock mugs in each row.

Ogtown sports club

Ogtown is going to have a new sports club.

The mayor wants to make sure that the people of Ogtown get the sort of sports club they want and need. He has asked everyone which sports they would like to be able to do at the club. Gathering information like this is called doing a **survey**. Here is the tally sheet showing the results of the survey.

cycling	////			
swimming	##// ##// ##//	////		
racketball	##// ##//	//		
stretch tum	##// ##//	////		
archery	//			
swivel body	##//	///		
stickball	##// ##//	///		
body bop	##//	////		
athletics	##// ##//	/		
kickball	##// ##// ##//	/		

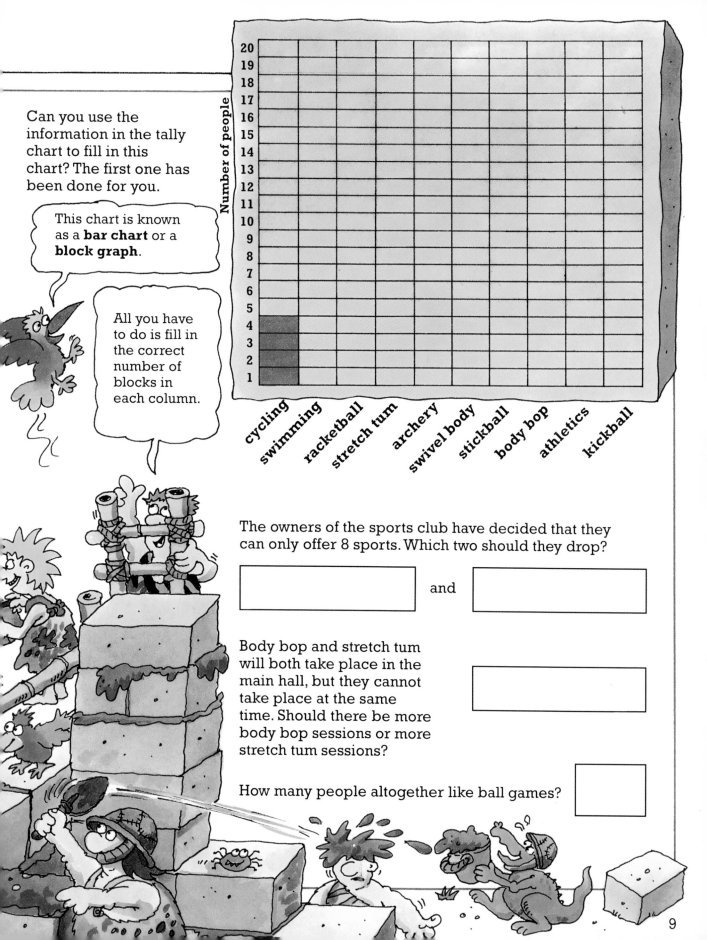

Can you use the information in the tally chart to fill in this chart? The first one has been done for you.

This chart is known as a **bar chart** or a **block graph**.

All you have to do is fill in the correct number of blocks in each column.

Number of people

cycling swimming racketball stretch tum archery swivel body stickball body bop athletics kickball

The owners of the sports club have decided that they can only offer 8 sports. Which two should they drop?

[ ] and [ ]

Body bop and stretch tum will both take place in the main hall, but they cannot take place at the same time. Should there be more body bop sessions or more stretch tum sessions?

[ ]

How many people altogether like ball games?

[ ]

9

Ogtown weather

Grandpa Og is very interested in the weather. He spends a lot of his time collecting weather data.

Remember, **data** is another word for information.

One of the things that Grandpa Og records is how much rain has fallen. He measures the rainfall in finger-widths, which are written "fw".

This list shows how much rain fell during each month of last year.

Last year's rainfall

January 5 fw
February 4 fw
March 5 fw
April 3 fw
May 5 fw
June 5 fw
July 6 fw
August 6 fw
September 5 fw
October 6 fw
November 7 fw
December 5 fw

Grandpa Og can show this information on a chart called a **bar-line chart**.

All he has to do is draw a line straight up from the black dot at the bottom. He stops when the top of the line is opposite the correct number of finger-widths.

Grandpa Og has drawn the first line. Can you help him by drawing the rest? Remember to use only the black dots.

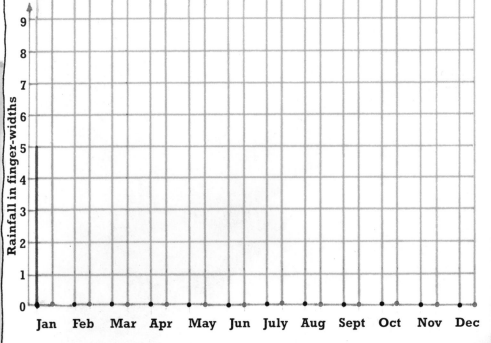

Grandpa has been collecting information about the weather since he was a boy. He has been recording the rainfall for years.

Below, you can see the rainfall for the year before last.

Use a different pen and draw a second set of lines on the chart. Start on the red dot. Now you can compare the rainfall in two different years.

Rainfall for year before last

January 4 fw

February 6 fw

March 4 fw

April 2 fw

May 3 fw

June 4 fw

July 6 fw

August 5 fw

September 3 fw

October 8 fw

November 6 fw

December 6 fw

When you have drawn in both sets of lines on the chart, see if you can help Grandpa Og solve these problems.

Grandpa Og wants to invite his brother to Ogtown for a visit. His brother hates rain. Which would be the best month to invite him?

Can you help Grandpa Og decide which was the wettest month last year?

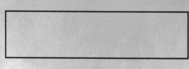

Which was the wettest month the year before last?

This sort of chart is very useful for comparing one set of information with another similar set of information.

Mrs. Og's notebook

Mrs. Og has a very busy life. There are so many things going on that she writes them all down in a notebook.

The problem with this is that the things she writes down are in no particular order and she keeps missing appointments and forgetting to buy things. Once she even forgot Mr. Og's birthday!

This is Mrs. Og's notebook.

June

Meet Mrs. Ig for lunch on the 10th.

20th - Visit Uncle Gog

Pay phone bill on the 11th.

Town Fair - 19th

30th - Go to the library

Zog's birthday on the 25th - buy present the day before.

3rd - Parents' evening at Zog and Mog's school.

Dentist on the 9th.

6th - Picnic with the Ugs.

Body bop every Tuesday.

Take Mog's pet lizard to the vet on the 16th.

Hair appointment on the 4th.

17th - Take car to be repaired

28th - Collect watch from Mr. Mendit's.

Mrs. Ug coming for coffee on the 14th.

Mr. Og decides to buy Mrs. Og a calendar. He thinks that this will be a much better way of writing everything down.

Can you put all the information in the notebook onto the calendar?

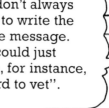

You don't always have to write the whole message. You could just write, for instance, "lizard to vet".

June

Sunday	Monday	Tuesday	Wednesday	Thursday	Friday	Saturday
		1	2	3	4	5
6	7	8	9	10	11	12
13	14	15	16 lizard to vet	17	18	19
20	21	22	23	24	25	26
27	28	29	30			

Can you see how much clearer the information looks when it is set out like this? A **calendar** is a sort of chart.

Mrs. Og has a friend in Igville whose name is Miss Stone. Miss Stone phones to invite her to Igville for the day.

Miss Stone has every Wednesday free except the 2nd.

Can you decide which day Mrs. Og can go to Igville and write it in on the calendar for her?

The grid game

How did he do that?

Mog and Zog are playing a grid game. Mog gives Zog the list below.

This is the picture Zog draws using this list.

A (4,8)

B (5,6)

C (7,5)

D (5,4)

E (4,1)

F (3,4)

G (1,5)

H (3,6)

Join H to A

Zog used the numbers to draw the dots on the grid. To find point A, Zog had to go across 4 and up 8.

He continued drawing and labelling all the points, then he joined them in alphabetical order. When he got to H he joined that back up to A.

Drawing in points or crosses on a grid or graph is sometimes called **plotting**.

Pairs of numbers like these are called **coordinates**.

Zog has drawn a picture for Mog. Can you write down the coordinates he needs to give her so that she can draw an identical picture?

Remember! The first number is how far across. The second number is how far up.

A
B
C
D
E
F
G
H
I
J
K
L
M
Join M to B

14

Mog and Zog have made up a grid puzzle for Grandpa Og. He is finding it rather difficult.

Can you help him out by plotting the coordinates and then joining them in alphabetical order?

A (3,10)   M (7,2)

B (5,5)   N (7,3)

C (7,5)   O (5,3)

D (8,7)   P (5,1)

E (7,9)   Q (3,1)

F (5,11)   R (3,2)

G (8,9)   S (4,2)

H (9,7)   T (4,3)

I (8,3)   U (2,8)

J (8,1)   V (1,8)

K (6,1)   W (1,9)

L (6,2)   X (2,10)

Join X to A

Mr. Og's garden

Mr. Og loves gardening. He grows flowers, fruit and vegetables.

This year Mr. Og is growing sunflowers. Each week he measures the height, in finger-widths (written "fw"), of one of the sunflowers and writes it on the rock below.

Height in finger-widths (vertical axis: 0, 10, 20, 30, 40, 50, 60, 70, 80, 90, 100, 110, 120, 130, 140, 150, 160, 170, 180)

(horizontal axis: week 1, week 2, week 3, week 4, week 5, week 6, week 7, week 8, week 9, week 10, week 11, week 12)

Mr. Og thinks a graph might show his tall sunflower's growth more clearly. He's done the first 2 weeks. Can you fill in the rest?

To draw in the first cross, Mr. Og went across one (for week 1) and up 0 (for zero finger-widths). He marked in the second cross in the same way then drew a line between the two crosses.

This sort of graph is called a **line graph**. Line graphs are very useful for looking at the way things change over time.

Week 1   0 fw
Week 2   10 fw
Week 3   20 fw
Week 4   30 fw
Week 5   50 fw
Week 6   70 fw
Week 7   100 fw
Week 8   120 fw
Week 9   140 fw
Week 10 160 fw
Week 11 170 fw
Week 12 180 fw

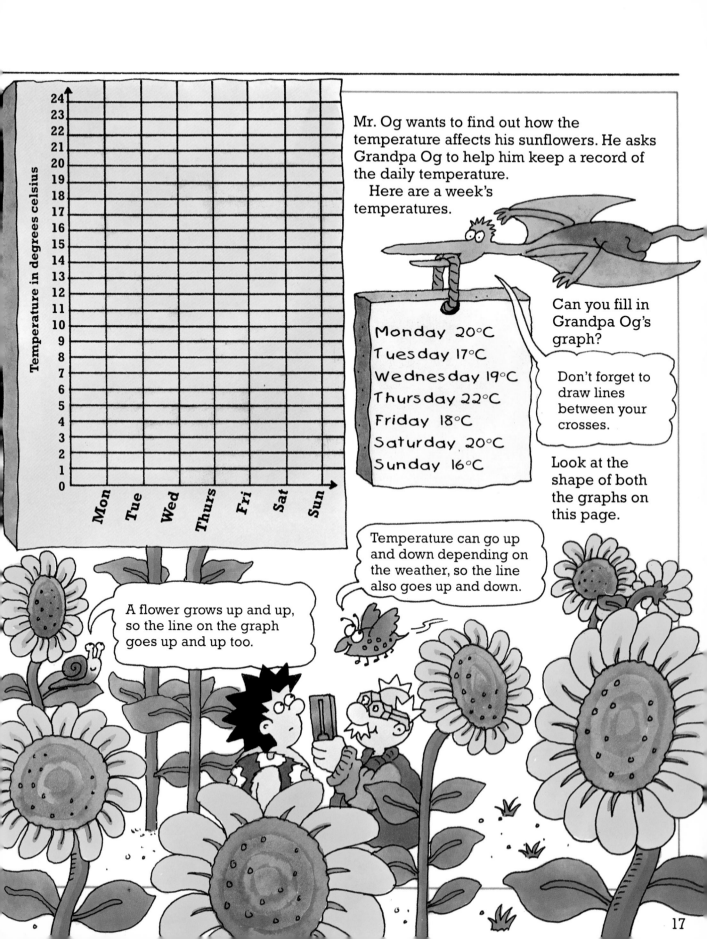

Temperature in degrees celsius

24 23 22 21 20 19 18 17 16 15 14 13 12 11 10 9 8 7 6 5 4 3 2 1 0

Mon Tue Wed Thurs Fri Sat Sun

Mr. Og wants to find out how the temperature affects his sunflowers. He asks Grandpa Og to help him keep a record of the daily temperature.

Here are a week's temperatures.

Monday 20°C
Tuesday 17°C
Wednesday 19°C
Thursday 22°C
Friday 18°C
Saturday 20°C
Sunday 16°C

Can you fill in Grandpa Og's graph?

Don't forget to draw lines between your crosses.

Look at the shape of both the graphs on this page.

Temperature can go up and down depending on the weather, so the line also goes up and down.

A flower grows up and up, so the line on the graph goes up and up too.

The one-price shop

Grandma Og's friend, Mrs. Mig, owns a shop called The One-Price shop. She called it this because she decided it would be easier to manage if she sold everything at the same price.

Mrs. Mig is now quite old, but when she was young, the price of each of the items in her shop was 2 bones.

This was the cost of various numbers of items:

1 item cost 2 bones
2 items cost 4 bones
3 items cost 6 bones
4 items cost 8 bones
5 items cost 10 bones

You can plot this information on the graph below. First of all, just draw all the crosses. Do not join them.

When you have drawn all the crosses, get a ruler. Use the ruler to draw a line through all the crosses.

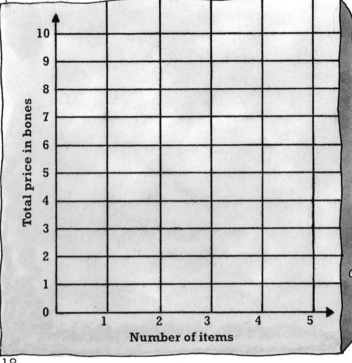

Can you see that all the crosses lie in a straight line?

The reason they are in a straight line is because the difference between all the crosses is exactly the same. As each item is added, the total amount goes up by two bones.

All times tables make a straight line graph like this.

Since those days, the price of everything in the One-Price Shop has gone up.

Now all the goods cost 13 bones each. Mrs. Mig isn't very good at multiplying by 13 any more, so she has made herself a graph.

Mrs. Mig has worked out that five 13s are 65 and has drawn a cross in the correct place. She knows that one 13 is 13 and has drawn a cross there too.

If you take your ruler and, very carefully, draw a line between the middles of the two crosses, you should be able to work out what two, three and four 13s are.

Work out the cost of the items in each of these baskets and write the total on each label.

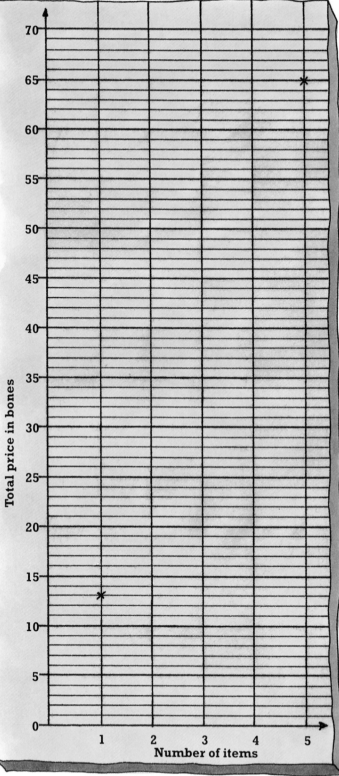

Mrs. Mig decides to have a sale. Everything is reduced to 8 bones.

Plot the sale prices on the graph and draw a line between them. Now draw another label on each basket and write down the sale price in it.

Five 8s are 40 and one 8 is 8.

19

The tourist information office

In the summer, Ogtown is visited by many tourists.

Mrs. Og works part-time in the Tourist Information Office. She gives visitors a brochure all about Ogtown and the surrounding countryside. These are the pages in the brochure that show all the hotels in the area.

The Old Brontosaurus is a big hotel near the town's railway station. It has an excellent restaurant.

The Old Brontosaurus

Swamp Grange has 10 bedrooms and is situated in beautiful, boggy countryside. All the rooms have delightful views.

Swamp Grange

Bumbleberry Lodge is a pretty little bed and breakfast hotel. It is situated on the main road into town.

Bumbleberry Lodge

The Mammoth is the largest hotel in Ogtown. It is also the only hotel with a swimming pool.

The Mammoth

The Dinosaur's Head is an old inn in the middle of town. Breakfast, lunch and dinner are all available.

The Dinosaur's Head

Stone House is down a quiet lane near the main street. Guests usually eat in town as dinner is not served here.

Stone House

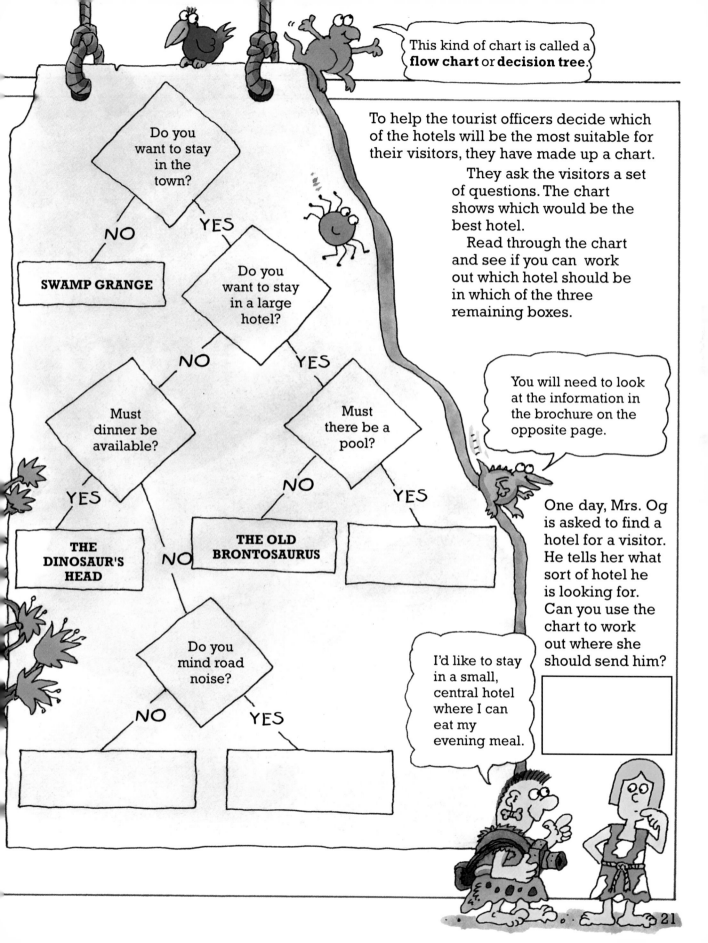

This kind of chart is called a **flow chart** or **decision tree**.

To help the tourist officers decide which of the hotels will be the most suitable for their visitors, they have made up a chart.

They ask the visitors a set of questions. The chart shows which would be the best hotel.

Read through the chart and see if you can work out which hotel should be in which of the three remaining boxes.

You will need to look at the information in the brochure on the opposite page.

One day, Mrs. Og is asked to find a hotel for a visitor. He tells her what sort of hotel he is looking for. Can you use the chart to work out where she should send him?

I'd like to stay in a small, central hotel where I can eat my evening meal.

Flow chart boxes:

Do you want to stay in the town?
- NO → **SWAMP GRANGE**
- YES → Do you want to stay in a large hotel?
  - NO → Must dinner be available?
    - YES → **THE DINOSAUR'S HEAD**
    - NO → Do you mind road noise?
      - NO → [ ]
      - YES → [ ]
  - YES → Must there be a pool?
    - NO → **THE OLD BRONTOSAURUS**
    - YES → [ ]

Ogtown's tourist attractions

There are many tourist attractions in Ogtown.

The town has an excellent modern art gallery.

There is a very good theatre called the Oggitorium. This week, the Jumping Jogtown Jugglers are putting on a show.

Visitor survey

The senior information officer at the town's Information Office thinks it would be useful to know the main reason why visitors choose to visit Ogtown.

She conducts a survey of one hundred visitors. These are the results.

Main reasons for visiting Ogtown

Gallery |||| |||| |||| ||||

Oggitorium |||| |||| ||||

Fantasy Museum |||| ||||
|||| |||| |||| |||| ||||

Dinostore ||||

Countryside |||| |||| |||| |||| ||||

Turn back to pages 8 and 9 to remind yourself about bar charts.

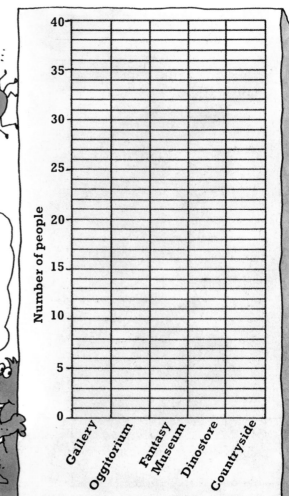

Can you help her use this information to make a bar chart?

Lots of people visit the Fantasy Museum of the Future.

There are shops to suit all tastes. Most people visit Horrids, the Dinostore, at least once.

Some people come to Ogtown to walk in the surrounding countryside.

Mrs. Og's great idea

Mrs. Og thinks of another way of showing this information. She explains it to the senior information officer.

She has drawn a circle and divided it into twenty segments. Each segment represents five people.

Twenty people said that the main reason they came to Ogtown was to visit the gallery. So, she has filled in four segments because four 5s are twenty.

Can you fill in the correct number of segments for each of the tourist attractions in Ogtown, using a different crayon for each one?

Now label each of the different sections.

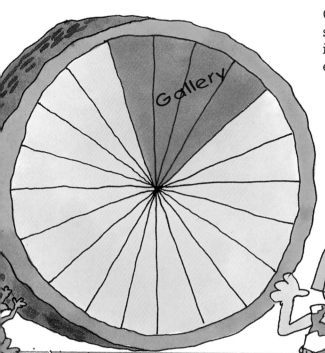

Gallery

There is an easy way to know how many segments to fill in. There are five tally marks in each group, so all you have to do is count the number of groups of tally marks then fill in the same number of segments.

This is called a **pie chart**. Pie charts are very handy for showing shares of the whole amount.

The wedding

The Ogs are at a family wedding.

Fern Og, the daughter of Mr. Og's brother, Trug, is getting married.

It has been many years since the whole family last got together. Unfortunately, no one can remember who anyone else is.

They all introduce themselves to one another, but it is still very confusing.

Grandpa has decided that the best way to show who's who is to draw a chart called a **family tree**.

I am Fern. I am Swamp's sister and Trug and Stella's daughter.

I am Flug. I am married to Mr. Og's sister.

I am Stella. My daughter is getting married.

My name is Trug. I am one of Grandpa Og's sons. I have 2 children.

My name is Swamp. I am married. Petra is my aunt.

I am Petra. I am Grandpa Og's daughter. I have 1 child.

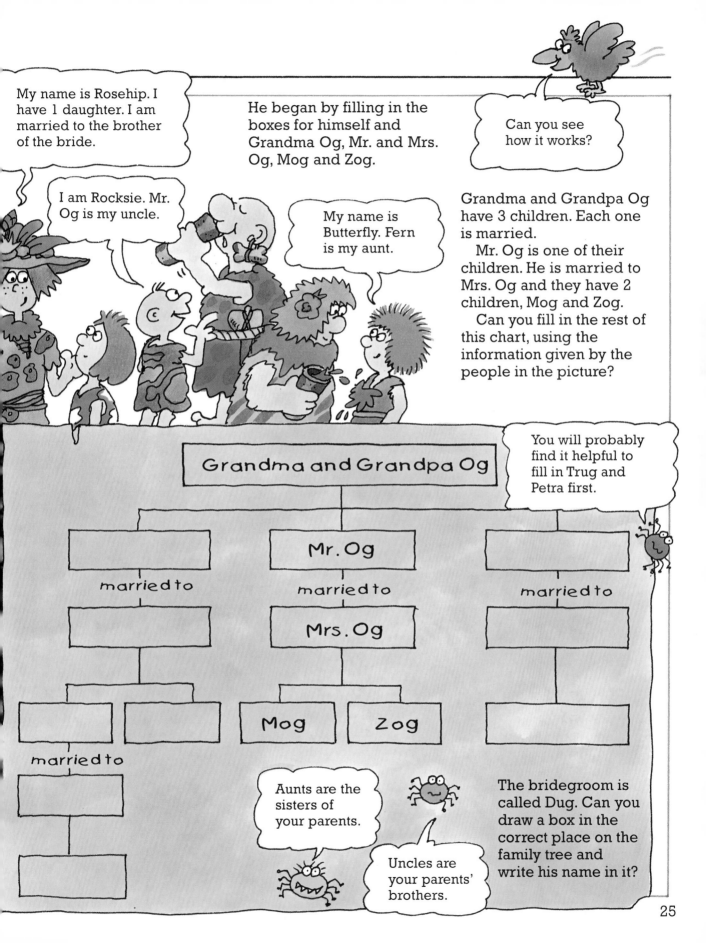

My name is Rosehip. I have 1 daughter. I am married to the brother of the bride.

I am Rocksie. Mr. Og is my uncle.

My name is Butterfly. Fern is my aunt.

He began by filling in the boxes for himself and Grandma Og, Mr. and Mrs. Og, Mog and Zog.

Can you see how it works?

Grandma and Grandpa Og have 3 children. Each one is married.

Mr. Og is one of their children. He is married to Mrs. Og and they have 2 children, Mog and Zog.

Can you fill in the rest of this chart, using the information given by the people in the picture?

Grandma and Grandpa Og

married to

Mr. Og

married to

Mrs. Og

married to

Mog   Zog

married to

You will probably find it helpful to fill in Trug and Petra first.

Aunts are the sisters of your parents.

Uncles are your parents' brothers.

The bridegroom is called Dug. Can you draw a box in the correct place on the family tree and write his name in it?

A treasure hunt

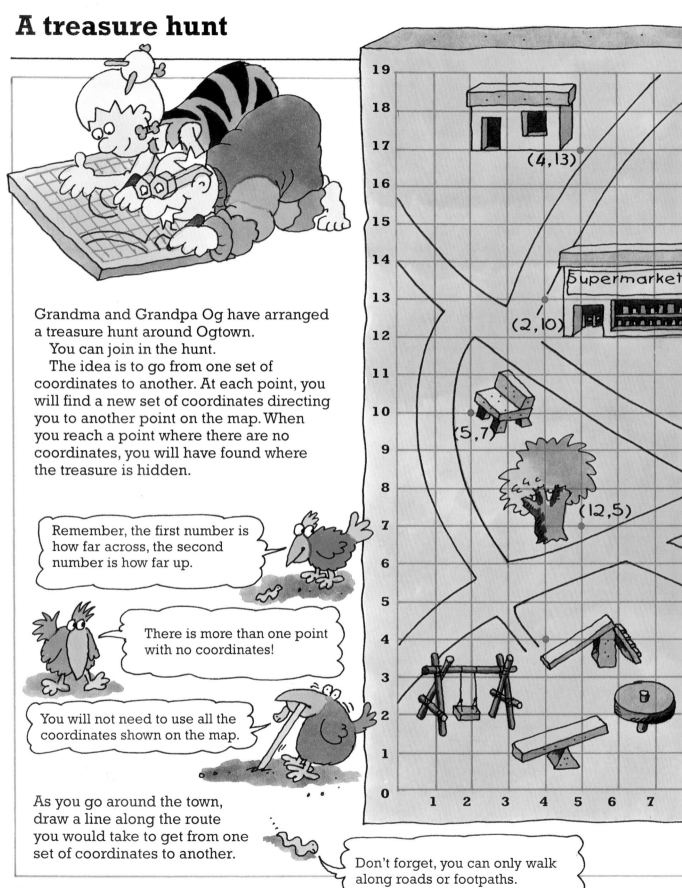

Grandma and Grandpa Og have arranged a treasure hunt around Ogtown.

You can join in the hunt.

The idea is to go from one set of coordinates to another. At each point, you will find a new set of coordinates directing you to another point on the map. When you reach a point where there are no coordinates, you will have found where the treasure is hidden.

Remember, the first number is how far across, the second number is how far up.

There is more than one point with no coordinates!

You will not need to use all the coordinates shown on the map.

As you go around the town, draw a line along the route you would take to get from one set of coordinates to another.

Don't forget, you can only walk along roads or footpaths.

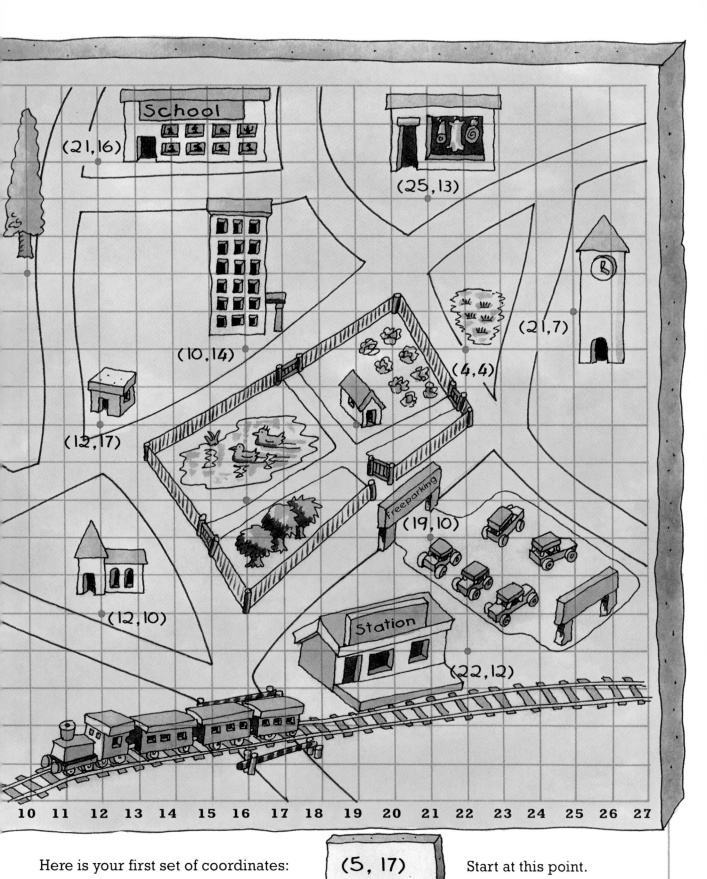

School

(21,16)

(25,13)

(21,7)

(10,14)

(4,4)

(12,17)

Freeparking

(19,10)

(12,10)

Station

(22,12)

10 11 12 13 14 15 16 17 18 19 20 21 22 23 24 25 26 27

Here is your first set of coordinates: (5, 17)   Start at this point.

27

Answers

Page 2

What are charts and graphs?

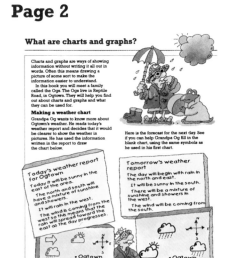

Charts and graphs are ways of showing information without writing it all out in words. Often this means drawing a picture of some sort to make the information easier to understand.

In this book you will meet a family called the Ogs. The Ogs live in Reptile Road, in Ogtown. They will help you find out about charts and graphs and what they can be used for.

Making a weather chart

Grandpa Og wants to know more about Ogtown's weather. He reads today's weather report and decides that it would be clearer to show the weather in pictures. He has used the information written in the report to draw the chart below.

Here is the forecast for the next day. See if you can help Grandpa Og fill in the blank chart, using the same symbols as he used in his first chart.

Today's weather report for Ogtown

Today it will be sunny in the east of the area.
The north and south will have a mixture of sunshine and showers.
It will rain in the west.
The wind is coming from the west so this means that the rain will spread toward the east as the day progresses.

Tomorrow's weather report
The day will begin with rain in the north and east.
It will be sunny in the south.
There will be a mixture of sunshine and showers in the west.
The wind will be coming from the south.

Page 3

9 bikes and 13 trucks went by.

Page 5

Mrs. Og yellow flowers ||||| ||||| ||||| ||

Grandpa Og butterflies ||||| ||

Grandma Og spiders ||||| ||

Mr. Og dragonflies ||||

Zog Og red flowers ||||| ||||

Mog Og lizards ||||| |

The Ogs are on a nature watch in Fern Forest. Zog suggests they all make tally sheets for the plants or animals they like best. As soon as they spot one of the things they like, they make a tally mark on their sheets.

Can you help the Ogs fill in their tally sheets?

Pages 6 and 7

In the café

Mog and Zog often go to the Tyrannosaurus Rex Café in Ogtown. It is owned by their friend, Mr. Trog.

There are only four things on the food menu and four things on the drinks menu in the T-Rex Café.

Mr. Trog likes to keep a count of all the items he sells. He thinks that he is a very good artist. Instead of making a tally sheet, he prefers to draw a picture of everything that he sells.

This is what Mr. Trog sold yesterday.

Food	
Swampburger	17 pebbles
Brontoburger	19 pebbles
T-Rex Steak	25 pebbles
Pterodactyl Pie	16 pebbles

Drinks	
Beetle Juice	10 pebbles
Slug Juice	9 pebbles
Glug Juice	12 pebbles
Bug Juice	11 pebbles

This sort of chart is called a **pictograph**.

Swamp-burger	
Bronto-burger	
T-Rex Steak	
Pterodactyl Pie	

What was the most popular meal?

Brontoburger

How many swampburgers were sold?

3

If Mr. Trog wanted to change one of the meals on the menu, which do you think he should choose?

Pterodactyl Pie

Mog and Zog decide to order a glass of juice. Mog has slug juice and Zog has glug juice.

So far today, including these drinks, Mr. Trog has sold 8 rock mugs of beetle juice, 4 rock mugs of slug juice, 7 rock mugs of glug juice and 10 rock mugs of bug juice.

Find some crayons and complete this pictograph by filling in the correct number of rock mugs in each row.

Beetle Juice

Slug Juice

Glug Juice

Bug Juice

Page 9

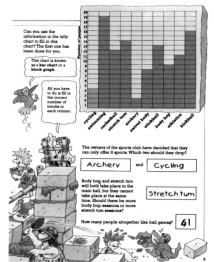

Can you use the information in the tally chart to fill in this chart? The first one has been done for you.

This chart is known as a **bar chart** or a **block graph**.

All you have to do is fill in the correct number of blocks in each column.

The owners of the sports club have decided that they can only offer 8 sports. Which two should they drop?

Archery and Cycling

Body bop and stretch turn will both take place in the main hall, but they cannot take place at the same time. Should there be more body bop sessions or more stretch turn sessions?

Stretch turn

How many people altogether like ball games? 41

28

Pages 10 and 11

Ogtown weather

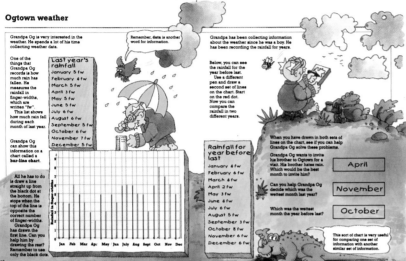

Page 13

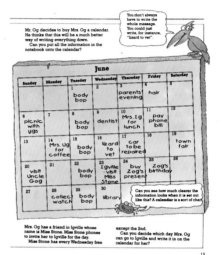

Pages 14 and 15

The grid game

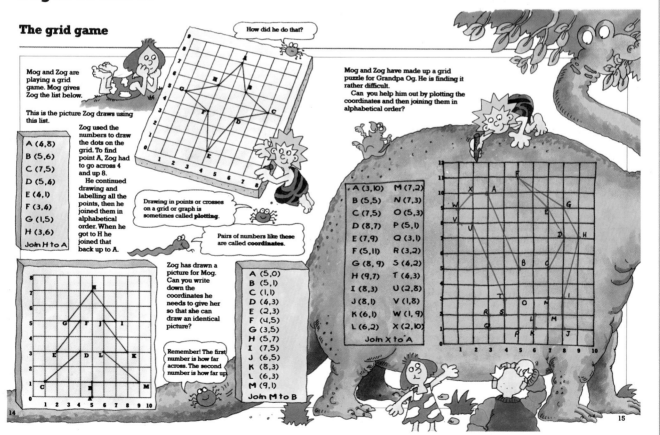

Mr. Og's garden

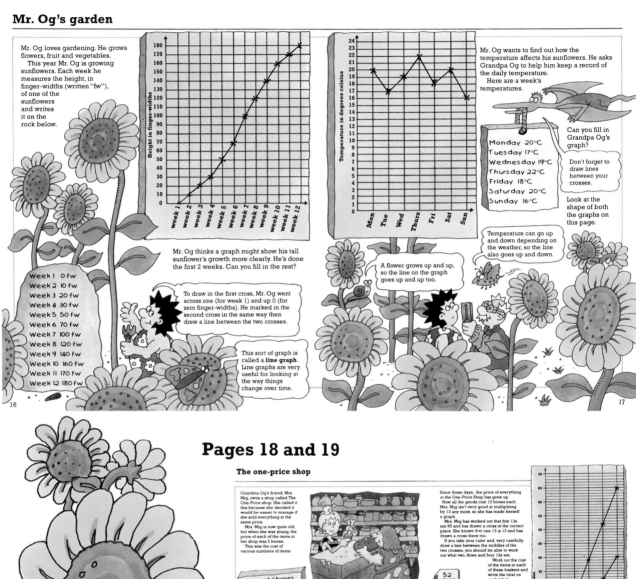

Mr. Og loves gardening. He grows flowers, fruit and vegetables.

This year Mr. Og is growing sunflowers. Each week he measures the height, in finger-widths (written "fw"), of one of the sunflowers and writes it on the rock below.

Mr. Og wants to find out how the temperature affects his sunflowers. He asks Grandpa Og to help him keep a record of the daily temperature.

Here are a week's temperatures.

Monday 20°C
Tuesday 17°C
Wednesday 19°C
Thursday 22°C
Friday 18°C
Saturday 20°C
Sunday 16°C

Can you fill in Grandpa Og's graph?

Don't forget to draw lines between your crosses.

Look at the shape of both the graphs on this page.

Mr. Og thinks a graph might show his tall sunflower's growth more clearly. He's done the first 2 weeks. Can you fill in the rest?

Temperature can go up and down depending on the weather, so the line also goes up and down.

A flower grows up and up, so the line on the graph goes up and up too.

To draw in the first cross, Mr. Og went across one (for week 1) and up 0 (for zero finger-widths). He marked in the second cross in the same way then drew a line between the two crosses.

This sort of graph is called a **line graph**. Line graphs are very useful for looking at the way things change over time.

Week 1   0 fw
Week 2   10 fw
Week 3   20 fw
Week 4   30 fw
Week 5   50 fw
Week 6   70 fw
Week 7   100 fw
Week 8   120 fw
Week 9   140 fw
Week 10 160 fw
Week 11 170 fw
Week 12 180 fw

16

17

Pages 18 and 19

The one-price shop

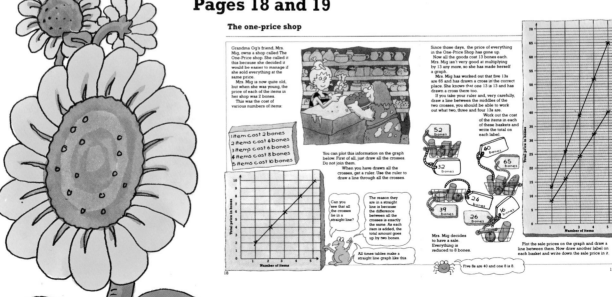

Grandma Og's friend, Mrs. Mig, owns a shop called The One-Price shop. She called it this because she decided it would be easier to manage if she sold everything at the same price.

Mrs. Mig is now quite old, but when she was young, the price of each of the items in her shop was 2 bones.

This was the cost of various numbers of items:

1 item cost 2 bones
2 items cost 4 bones
3 items cost 6 bones
4 items cost 8 bones
5 items cost 10 bones

You can plot this information on the graph below. First of all, just draw all the crosses. Do not join them.

When you have drawn all the crosses, get a ruler. Use the ruler to draw a line through all the crosses.

Since those days, the price of everything in the One-Price Shop has gone up. Now all the goods cost 13 bones each. Mrs. Mig isn't very good at multiplying by 13 any more, so she has made herself a graph.

Mrs. Mig has worked out that five 13s are 65 and has drawn a cross in the correct place. She knows that one 13 is 13 and has drawn a cross there too.

If you take your ruler and, very carefully, draw a line between the middles of the two crosses, you should be able to work out what two, three and four 13s are.

Can you see that all the crosses lie in a straight line?

The reason they are in a straight line is because the difference between all the crosses is exactly the same. As each item is added, the total amount goes up by two bones.

All times tables make a straight line graph like this.

Work out the cost of the items in each of these baskets and write the total on each label.

52 bones
60 bones
32 bones
65 bones
39 bones
24 bones
26 bones
16 bones

Mrs. Mig decides to have a sale. Everything is reduced to 8 bones.

Plot the sale prices on the graph and draw a line between them. Now draw another label on each basket and write down the sale price in it.

Five 8s are 40 and one 8 is 8.

18

19

Pages 20 and 21

The tourist information office

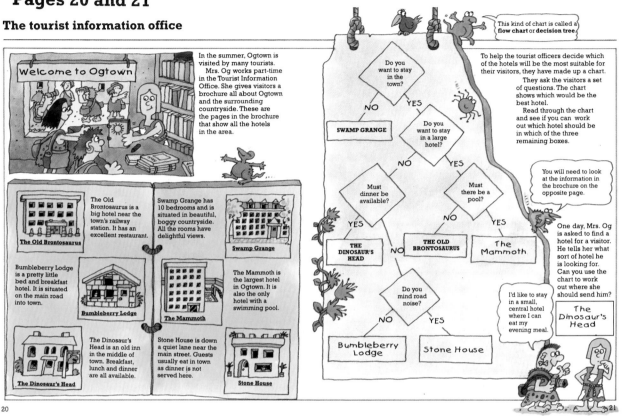

In the summer, Ogtown is visited by many tourists.

Mrs. Og works part-time in the Tourist Information Office. She gives visitors a brochure all about Ogtown and the surrounding countryside. These are the pages in the brochure that show all the hotels in the area.

The Old Brontosaurus is a big hotel near the town's railway station. It has an excellent restaurant.

The Old Brontosaurus

Swamp Grange has 10 bedrooms and is situated in beautiful, boggy countryside. All the rooms have delightful views.

Swamp Grange

Bumbleberry Lodge is a pretty little bed and breakfast hotel. It is situated on the main road into town.

Bumbleberry Lodge

The Mammoth is the largest hotel in Ogtown. It is also the only hotel with a swimming pool.

The Mammoth

The Dinosaur's Head is an old inn in the middle of town. Breakfast, lunch and dinner are all available.

The Dinosaur's Head

Stone House is down a quiet lane near the main street. Guests usually eat in town as dinner is not served here.

Stone House

This kind of chart is called a **flow chart** or **decision tree**.

To help the tourist officers decide which of the hotels will be the most suitable for their visitors, they have made up a chart.

They ask the visitors a set of questions. The chart shows which would be the best hotel.

Read through the chart and see if you can work out which hotel should be in which of the three remaining boxes.

You will need to look at the information in the brochure on the opposite page.

One day, Mrs. Og is asked to find a hotel for a visitor. He tells her what sort of hotel he is looking for. Can you use the chart to work out where she should send him?

I'd like to stay in a small, central hotel where I can eat my evening meal.

The Dinosaur's Head

Decision tree:
- Do you want to stay in the town?
  - NO → SWAMP GRANGE
  - YES → Do you want to stay in a large hotel?
    - NO → Must dinner be available?
      - YES → THE DINOSAUR'S HEAD
      - NO → Do you mind road noise?
        - NO → Bumbleberry Lodge
        - YES → Stone House
    - YES → Must there be a pool?
      - NO → THE OLD BRONTOSAURUS
      - YES → The Mammoth

20   21

Pages 22 and 23

Ogtown's tourist attractions

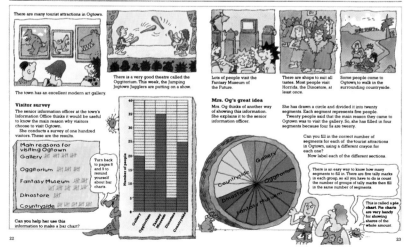

There are many tourist attractions in Ogtown.

The town has an excellent modern art gallery.

There is a very good theatre called the Oggitorium. This week, the Jumping Jogtown Jugglers are putting on a show.

Lots of people visit the Fantasy Museum of the Future.

There are shops to suit all tastes. Most people visit Horrids, the Dinostore, at least once.

Some people come to Ogtown to walk in the surrounding countryside.

Visitor survey
The senior information officer at the town's Information Office thinks it would be useful to know the main reason why visitors choose to visit Ogtown.

She conducts a survey of one hundred visitors. These are the results.

Main reasons for visiting Ogtown

Gallery 卌 卌 卌
Oggitorium 卌 卌
Fantasy Museum 卌 卌 卌 llll
Dinostore 卌 llll
Countryside 卌 卌 卌 卌 llll

Can you help her use this information to make a bar chart?

Turn back to pages 8 and 9 to remind yourself about bar charts.

Mrs. Og's great idea
Mrs. Og thinks of another way of showing this information. She explains it to the senior information officer.

She has drawn a circle and divided it into twenty segments. Each segment represents five people. Twenty people said that the main reason they came to Ogtown was to visit the gallery. So, she has filled in four segments because four 5s are twenty.

Can you fill in the correct number of segments for each of the tourist attractions in Ogtown, using a different crayon for each one?

Now label each of the different sections.

There is an easy way to know how many segments to fill in. There are five tally marks in each group, so all you have to do is count the number of groups of tally marks then fill in the same number of segments.

This is called a **pie chart**. Pie charts are very handy for showing share of the whole amount.

22   23

Page 25

Pages 26 and 27

A treasure hunt

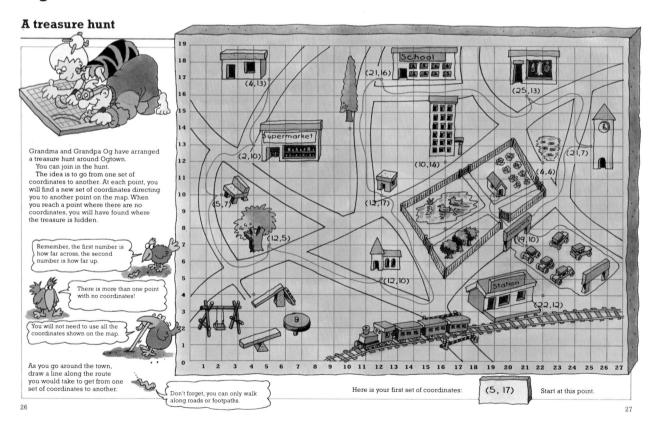

Grandma and Grandpa Og have arranged a treasure hunt around Ogtown.

You can join in the hunt.

The idea is to go from one set of coordinates to another. At each point, you will find a new set of coordinates directing you to another point on the map. When you reach a point where there are no coordinates, you will have found where the treasure is hidden.

Remember, the first number is how far across, the second number is how far up.

There is more than one point with no coordinates!

You will not need to use all the coordinates shown on the map.

As you go around the town, draw a line along the route you would take to get from one set of coordinates to another.

Don't forget, you can only walk along roads or footpaths.

Here is your first set of coordinates: (5, 17) Start at this point.

The treasure is hidden at (19,10).